KAREN WALLACE

Scarlette Beane

Illustrated by JON BERKELEY

Dial Books for Young Readers   New York

When Mrs. Beane
first saw her
daughter's face, it was
as red as a beet, and
the ends of her fingers
were green.

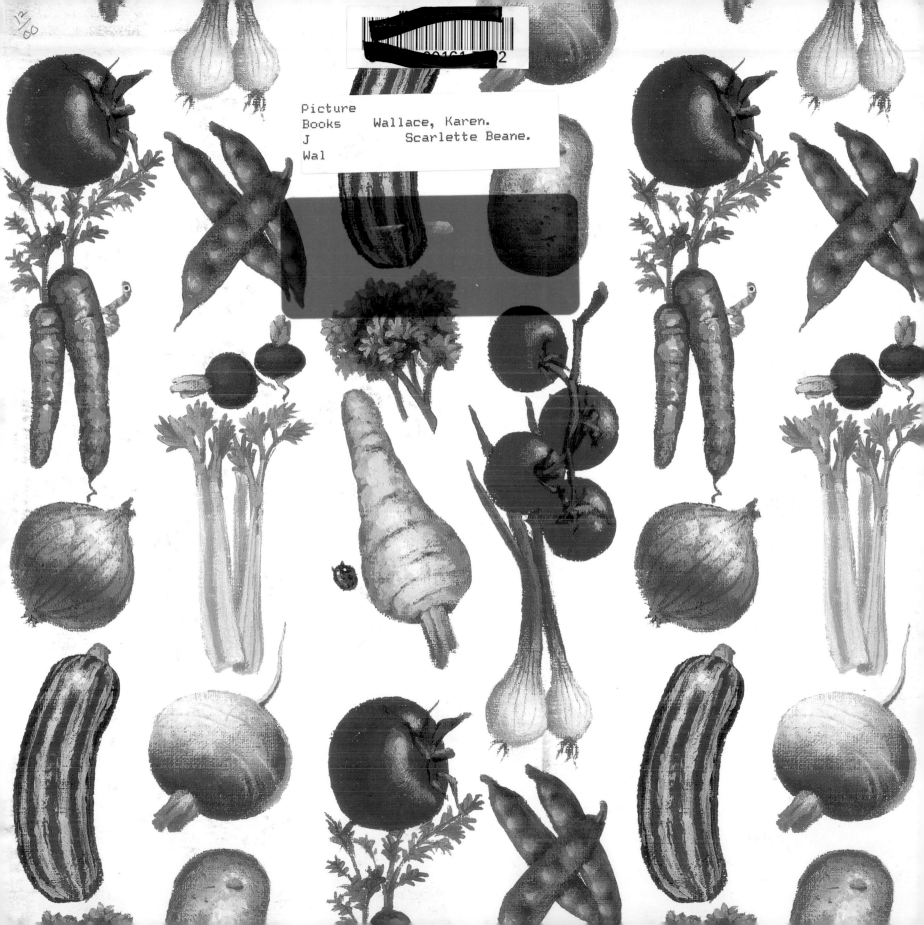

To Innes,
who taught me how to grow vegetables. K.W.

For my girls, Xaali and Lily. J.B.

First published in the United States in 2000 by
Dial Books for Young Readers
A division of Penguin Putnam Inc.
345 Hudson Street • New York, New York 10014

Published in Great Britain by Oxford University Press
Great Clarendon Street, Oxford OX2 6DP England

Library of Congress Cataloging in Publication Data
Wallace, Karen.
Scarlette Beane / Karen Wallace; illustrated by Jon Berkeley.—1st ed.
p. cm.
Summary: When family members give five-year-old Scarlette a garden,
she succeeds in growing gigantic vegetables and creating something wonderful.
ISBN 0-8037-2475-6
[1. Gardening—Fiction. 2. Vegetables—Fiction.] I. Berkeley, Jon, ill. II. Title.
PZ7.W1568Sc 2000
[Fic]—dc21 98-47173 CIP AC

The artwork is rendered in acrylic on textured paper.

Scarlette lay in her stroller and listened to the flowers grow.

And when she slept, she dreamed of doing something wonderful.

On her fifth birthday Grandfather Beane
gave Scarlette a vegetable garden.

"We shall call
her Scarlette,"
declared
Mrs. Beane.
"She will grow
tall and strong
and do something
wonderful."

Mr. and Mrs. Beane lived in
a house that looked like a
garden shed.

It was cozy and made of
wood, but it was very small.

So they worked outside
as much as they could.

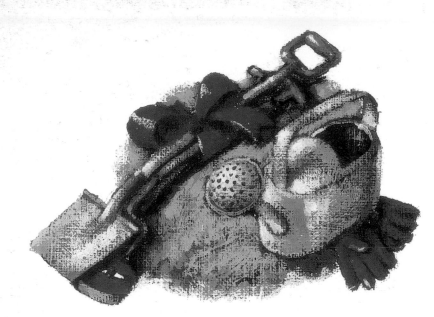

Her mother gave her a set of tools with wooden handles.

Her father built a wooden fence to keep out the rabbits.

And he made a white gate that Scarlette could open herself.

Scarlette loved her new garden.
She pulled up the weeds.

She dug in the soil until it was
as crumbly as chocolate cake.

She planted a row of
carrots, a row of onions,
and a row of parsley.

That night when she went to bed, the ends
of her fingers glowed like green lights.

The next morning Scarlette ran to her garden.

Her carrots were as huge
as tree trunks.

Her onions were as big
as hot-air balloons.

Her parsley was as thick
as a jungle.

Everyone in the village came to help.

They used bulldozers to dig up the carrots.

They drove forklifts
to carry the onions.

They cut the parsley
with chain saws.

Mrs. Beane's kitchen was too small for
so many vegetables. So she made soup
in a concrete mixer.

The house was too small for so many people.

So Mr. Beane served the soup in the garden. Everyone said it was the best soup ever.

And when it began to rain, they ate second helpings under the table.

That night Scarlette Beane
dreamed of something wonderful.

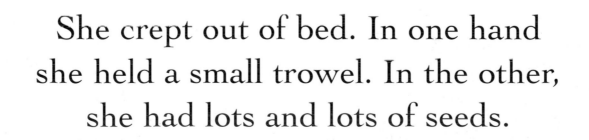

She crept out of bed. In one hand
she held a small trowel. In the other,
she had lots and lots of seeds.

High above the meadow,
the moon hung like a pearl
in the sky.

Scarlette dug a hole and put
all the seeds at the bottom.

As she covered them with
earth, the ends of her fingers
flashed like green stars.

The next morning the sun rose like
a huge golden coin. In the middle of the
meadow stood a castle made of vegetables.

It had turnip turrets
and a drawbridge held
up by corncobs.

A cucumber tower
stood at each corner.

Mr. Beane couldn't believe his eyes.
It was the house of his dreams.

Mrs. Beane kissed her
daughter's face.

"I knew you'd do
something wonderful,"
she whispered.

Scarlette Beane was so happy,
she turned as red as a beet.

And the ends of her fingers
sparkled like fireworks.

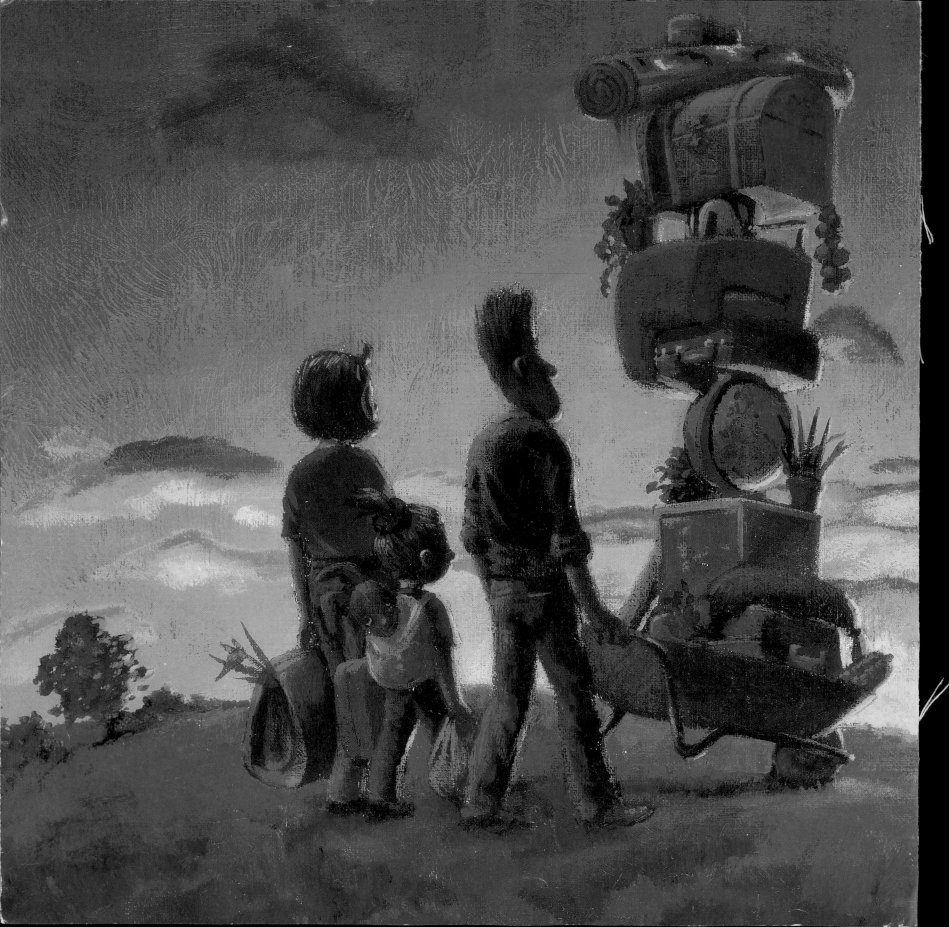